The Magic Moonberry
Jump Ropes

Dakari Hru

PICTURES BY E. B. Lewis

Dial Books for Young Readers *New York*

Glossary/Pronunciation Guide

dashiki (*dub-SHEE-kee*): a brightly colored, loose-fitting garment

Layla (*LAY-la*): Swahili name meaning "born at night"

Nubian (*NU-bee-an*): of or relating to Nubia, a region and ancient kingdom along the Nile River in Northeast Africa

Swahili (*Swa-HEE-lee*): a language spoken in much of East Africa

Zambezi (*Zam-BAY-zee*): the name of a river in Southeast Africa

Published by Dial Books for Young Readers
A Division of Penguin Books USA Inc.
375 Hudson Street
New York, New York 10014

Text copyright © 1996 by the Estate of Dakari Hru
Pictures copyright © 1996 by E. B. Lewis
All rights reserved
Typography by Amelia Lau Carling
Printed in Hong Kong
First Edition
1 3 5 7 9 10 8 6 4 2

Library of Congress Cataloging in Publication Data
Hru, Dakari, 1952–1994
The magic moonberry jump ropes /
by Dakari Hru; pictures by E. B. Lewis.—1st ed.   p.   cm.
Summary: Uncle Zambezi brings his two nieces jump ropes from Tanzania,
telling the girls that when they use the magic ropes, their wishes will come true.
ISBN 0-8037-1754-7 (trade).—ISBN 0-8037-1755-5 (library)
[1. Rope skipping—Fiction. 2. Afro-Americans—Fiction.
3. Uncles—Fiction.] I. Lewis, Earl B., ill. II. Title.
PZ7.H85614Mag   1996   [E]—dc20   94-49337   CIP   AC

The full-color artwork was prepared using watercolors.
It was then scanner-separated and reproduced as
red, blue, yellow, and black halftones.

In loving memory of my mother,
Vivian Stewart,
and for Tiani, Tyrie, and Terrelle,
my beloved godchildren
D. H.

To my best friend, Cheryl,
who never learned to jump
E. B. L.

April and her little sister Erica loved to jump Double Dutch on the
school playground. On the first day of summer vacation they asked
the neighborhood kids to join in, but they all said, "No!"

"I like to ride my bike," said Mandell.

"I like skateboarding," said Keesha.

And so April and Erica had to find a way to jump Double Dutch all by themselves. First they tied the ends of the ropes to the fence in the front yard. April turned the ropes while Erica jumped.

April sang while she turned,

> *Drum Lady, Drum Lady, do your duty.*
> *Drum for the lady with the great, big boody.*
> *She can wiggle, she can waddle, she can do a split.*
> *But I bet you five dollars that she can't do this:*
> *Lady on one foot, one foot, one foot,*
> *Lady on two feet, two feet, two feet...*

Erica did karate kicks while she jumped. The red beads in her braids were flying all around. Clap-a-click, clap-a-click, clap-a-click. Those beads kept perfect rhythm.

Suddenly the girls' little dog, Cha-Cha, came bursting out of the front door.

Cha-Cha ran straight to Erica and tried to chew her socks. Then she got tangled in the jump rope.

"Cha-Cha, move!" April yelled.

Erica lost her balance and fell right into her big sister's arms.
"That crazy dog," said Erica.

"We can't jump Double Dutch like this," April sighed. "We need more playmates."

"I know," said Erica. "Let's ask Carmen."

"What?" cried April. "She's only three years old. She can't jump Double Dutch!"

But the girls ran into the house to Carmen's room anyway.

"Hold this, Carmen," said Erica, placing the ropes in her baby sister's hands. Carmen laughed and squeezed the ropes tightly.

"Turn the ropes, Carmen," said April. So Carmen and Erica turned the ropes while April jumped.

Little Carmen turned the ropes wildly, hitting furniture and knocking toys to the floor.

The girls' parents ran into the room when they heard the noise.

"You can't jump rope with Carmen," Mother said. "She's too little."

Just then they heard the doorbell ring. "Uncle Zambezi!" the girls yelled as they ran to let him in.

Their uncle had just returned from a trip to Tanzania in East Africa, and he was coming by with gifts for his nieces. Uncle Zambezi stood tall, and his big dashiki made him look even taller. His hair hung around his face in Nubian locks and his eyes were as big as his smile.

Uncle Zambezi leaned over. "Give me a hug," he said to the three girls. "I missed you while I was away." He reached deep into his bag and pulled out some musical bells for Carmen. "I was going to keep these for my art gallery," he said, "but I told myself, no, Carmen needs them more." She shook the bells and giggled.

Then Uncle Zambezi looked at April and Erica. "Do you two still jump rope like there's no tomorrow?"

"Oh, yes!" April replied.

"Me too!" said Erica.

He reached in his bag and pulled out two rainbow-colored jump ropes. April's and Erica's eyes grew big with excitement when their uncle placed the beautiful jump ropes in their hands.

Uncle Zambezi explained, "These are magic moonberry jump ropes, a special gift to you from my friend Layla in Tanzania."

"Are they really magic, Uncle Zambezi?" asked Erica.

He grinned. "You bet they are! Layla dyed them by hand. She used indigo, sunflower—and moonberries. You might call them cranberries, but these are special ones, just like Layla is special. Her name means 'born at night' in Swahili. She and her extra-beautiful cranberries get their power from the moon, so she calls them moonberries."

"What do magic moonberry jump ropes do, Uncle Zambezi?" April wanted to know.

"When you jump, they'll grant your wish, of course! Try them and see," he said.

April and Erica gave Uncle Zambezi a big hug and thanked him for the gifts. Then they pulled him right outside to jump with their new ropes. Miss Bessie May leaned out from her front porch to watch all the fun. Old Mr. Hicks stopped watering his lawn to look. Cha-Cha wagged her tail and barked.

Uncle Zambezi and Erica turned the ropes while April jumped. Uncle Zambezi sang,

> *Nubian Princess, turn around.*
> *Nubian Princess, touch the ground.*
> *Nubian Princess, tie your shoe.*
> *These ropes will grant a wish for you!*

"I have a wish," Erica said as she changed places with April. With her red beads clicking, Erica jumped in and sang,

> *Not last night, but the night before,*
> *Two new friends came knocking at my door.*
> *Then, then I let them in.*
> *We jumped rope again and again.*

Suddenly a big moving van pulled up to the vacant house across the street. April, Erica, and Uncle Zambezi watched openmouthed as the moving men began to unload boxes and lamps and two kid-size bikes. Then a blue car pulled up behind the moving van and out jumped a man, a lady, a boy with a football in his hands, and a girl.

"Our new friends!" exclaimed April.

"Uncle Zambezi," Erica said, hopping up and down, "did these jump ropes really grant my wish?"

Uncle Zambezi just smiled and winked. "Have fun," he said as he went back in the house.

The new kids waved to April and Erica, and the girls went over to say hello. April and Erica introduced themselves and asked right away if they jumped rope.

"I'm Takara Brown," said the girl. "And, yes! I love to jump rope."

"Not me, no way," said her brother. "I'm the Bammer! I play football." Bammer looked straight at Erica and said, "Those red beads are right on time!"

"Want to play with us?" April asked as Erica rolled her eyes.

Takara and Bammer asked their parents. "Yes," said Mrs. Brown, "you might as well play while the movers unload all the furniture and boxes."

April and Erica wanted to jump rope with Takara. Bammer asked Mandell if he liked football. The three girls jumped Double Dutch with the magic moonberry jump ropes while the boys tossed the football around.

"Here's a rhyme that I made up," Erica said. She sang,

Jump Takara, jump Takara, touch the sky.
Jump Takara, jump Takara, you're so fly.

"I have one," said Takara. Erica jumped into the ropes and Takara sang,

> Down in the valley where the green grass grows,
> There sat Erica, sweet as a rose.
> She sang, she sang, she sang so sweet.
> Along came Bammer and kissed her on the cheek.

"Oh, no!" Erica screamed and jumped out of the ropes. "I don't like boys."

Takara and April laughed. April jumped in and did the limbo.
Next Erica sang,

> *April, April, set the table.*
> *Just as fast as you are able.*
> *Don't forget the red...*

The ropes turned faster.

> *hot...*

They turned even faster.

> *pepper!*

Miss Bessie May danced off her front porch and swayed her hips to the rhythm. Old Mr. Hicks clapped his hands in time to the turning ropes. Mandell left Bammer with the football and did the wheelbarrow with Keesha. Cha-Cha ran to pull at everyone's socks.

The block was hotter than April's red peppers—hotter than Erica's red beads. The sisters switched places without missing a beat.

Even Bammer felt the magic. He dropped his football and jumped
into the ropes with Erica. And April sang,

> *Two in the middle and two at the end.*
> *Two jump out and two jump in.*
> *Two good sisters with two good friends.*
> *Two in the middle and two at the end!*

Author's Note

April and Erica's jump ropes are made from sisal (SYE-sul), a plant fiber that is found in the leaves of a yucca-like plant in the agave (uh-GUH-vee) family. Sisal, a source of jump ropes in Africa, is also used to make brushes, marine rope, and shipping twine. The city of Tanga (TANG-guh), in Tanzania, East Africa, is Africa's largest producer of sisal.

Raw sisal is usually creamy white and is often dyed bright colors to make decorative objects such as hats, mats, purses, and rugs. In Tanzania, parts of trees—bark, leaves, and even sap—can be used to produce the dyes. For instance, peach tree leaves will produce a yellow color. Many plants are also used to produce natural dyes; the following are all grown locally in Tanzania:

Name	Color
cranberry	yellow to red
henna	orange-red
bloodroot	reddish-orange
indigo	brown to blue
sunflower	yellow

While one of the jump rope rhymes in this story, "Jump Takara," is my own creation, most of these rhymes are traditional ones that have been handed down through several generations. I visited my very young cousins in Fort Dix, New Jersey, and Pittsburgh, Pennsylvania, to learn these rhymes from them. "Drum Lady" is direct from my young cousins in Pittsburgh; "Down in the valley" is another traditional rhyme.

I changed the words in four of the rhymes to fit the characters in my story. "Nubian Princess" was adapted from "Teddy Bear, Teddy Bear, turn around." "April, April, set the table" was adapted from the traditional rhyme "Mabel, Mabel, set the table." "Two in the middle and two at the end" was also adapted from the traditional jump rope rhyme of the same name.

"Not last night, but the night before" is from my childhood. We used to say,

> *"Not last night, but de night before,*
> *Twenty-five robbers came knockin' at my door.*
> *Den, den (then, then), I let 'em in—*
> *Hit 'em in de head wit' a rollin' pin."*

The version in this story was adapted to express Erica's wish.

I hope your jump rope experiences are as fun-filled as those of my real-life cousins April, Erica, and Carmen.